A LAST WISH FOR LARRY

JEFFREY WU

A LAST WISH
FOR LARRY

Illustrations by Zachariah Parks

T&C Books

ISBN: 1502584506
ISBN 13: 9781502584502

Inspired by a true story

I used to greet every person who passed through my three doorless doorways. In the early days they all smiled politely and inquired about my health. When the inquiries turned into tight-lipped nods and then into quick two-fingered waves, I realized that the partially partitioned stretch of corridor which was to me an office was to everyone else a shortcut, one as well-worn as an old backwoods Indian trail. I started to keep my head down and listen for those who were likely to be looking for me, much to the energy-conserving relief of those who were not. An unhurried, heavy-footed shuffle, for instance, meant that Sam, the file room clerk, was about to deliver another stray lab report along with his oft-repeated apology, "Sorry, Doc, found another one!" Mr. Leroy, the part-time minister and full-time custodian, announced the arrival of his trusty push-broom not so much with his footsteps as with the four bar musical phrase that he whistled hour after hour and day after day like a cheerful little songbird. My medical assistant Nan, on the other hand, approached with such cat-like stealth that I never knew she was in my office until she slammed another chart onto my desk, a nerve-jangling ritual that punctuated my day like a series of randomly misplaced exclamation points.

Then there was the rapid-fire click-click-click of Barbara Morgan's high heels on the linoleum floor, a sound which usually clicked through one doorway and out the other, much to my relief. There was no such luck this early autumn morning, though; those determined high heels came to an abrupt and decisive stop right in front of my desk, and I knew that Barbara knew that I was pretending to be unaware that she was standing there, smiling the patient smile of someone who knows that their presence will have to be acknowledged eventually. I continued to stare at the next patient's chart, but it was no use. I looked up, feigning an expression of surprise for a brief moment before deciding not to bother.

"What's up, Barbara?" I sighed.

Barbara smiled at me a few more seconds before answering, which meant that she was about to deliver me a great deal of work. "I'd like you to meet a very, very nice young man," she finally said. "I'm sure your next patient can wait a minute or two."

I stood up and, with a not very subtle glance at my watch, replied, "I'm already an hour behind, so I guess another minute or two won't make a difference."

I walked down the hall slowly to give Barbara a chance to tell me about the patient, though in truth I also derived a petty bit of pleasure from slowing Barbara down from her usual zealous pace. As we went on our little stroll, I tried to let go of my momentary aggravation and admit how much I had come to admire Barbara, both as a clinician and as a person. She had grown up in a family of alcoholics, lived with an alcoholic husband just long enough to bring into the world a pair of feisty boys, and then from the rubble of her marriage turned herself into a first-rate nurse practitioner. Barbara could have done very well at a private practice here in Mississippi or back in her native Texas, but she devoted herself instead to the incarcerated in our local prison and to the incapacitated in our windowless little public health clinic. Before my arrival, there hadn't been an internist at the clinic for three years, and Barbara had gamely done her best to hold the fort for thousands of chronically ill patients. Barbara seemed familiar from the moment I met her, and then one day it hit me; the movie "Steel Magnolias" had been in the theaters recently, and Barbara was our own Miz M'Lynn, the character played by Sally Field - clear-eyed, plain-spoken, loyal, and fiercely protective, a petite but iron-willed force of nature.

It only took Barbara twenty-five feet of corridor to summarize the patient's story. Sixteen year old black male who two years ago had been in the wrong place at the wrong time on the mean streets of Memphis. Gunshot wounds to the abdomen. Hours of trauma surgery. Umpteen units of blood - one of them tainted with HIV. Now starting to feel sick enough that he had asked his sister to take care of him. Needs a doctor rather than a nurse practitioner because of his level of illness.

"Of course," I agreed, referring to her final comment. "But he's sixteen. Clay should take care of him."

Barbara's smile told me that escape was not an option. "Dr. Cooper feels that a teenager with HIV belongs in adult medicine, not pediatrics," she said. "Besides, I want you to take care of this young man, not Clay." She punctuated her statement by poking me gently but firmly in the chest with her index finger.

I considered Barbara's remarks for a moment, acting as if I or anyone else could actually oppose her will. "All right," I agreed. "I'll take the case. What's his name?"

"Larry," Barbara replied with a satisfied smile. "He's here with his sister, Luanne. I know you'll like them. They're both very, very nice." Barbara handed me Larry's chart, spun around, and went off to save another soul, her high heels, released from the weight of my slow pace, accelerating as they went click-click-clicking down the hall.

I walked into Barbara's office and introduced myself. Larry was a rail of a boy, not unusually thin for a sixteen year old but with a touch of hollowness in his cheeks. Under his baggy sweat-shirt and jeans and his flat-billed baseball cap it was hard for me to detect any other signs of wasting. Larry avoided making eye contact at first, but when he finally mumbled, "Hey, Doc," and looked up at me I was struck by the playful curiosity in his dark brown eyes.

Larry was leaning gently against his sister, who in turn rested her hand protectively on Larry's forearm. Unlike her brother, Luanne was quick to make eye contact. Her gaze was shrewder than Larry's but not unkind. She made a quick study of me and asked, "Can you help my brother?"

I didn't answer Luanne's question right away. In some ways, taking care of someone with AIDS was simple in those days because there wasn't much treatment to offer; all we had was one antiretroviral medication, AZT, along with a couple of antibiotics for AIDS-related opportunistic infections. On the other hand, that same lack of treatment options made taking care of AIDS patients not only difficult but mostly futile.

The real reason I hesitated, however, was that I had never really been in charge of an AIDS patient. For that matter, I hadn't been in charge of many patients, period. Just a few months earlier, I had been patrolling the floors of a Boston teaching hospital, walking, as did my fellow senior residents, with a bit of a swag-ger, knowing that we had proven ourselves in a grueling internal medicine program. In our final weeks, as some of us prepared to join private practices and others awaited the transition to subspecialty fellowships, I flew to Mississippi to visit my girlfriend, Jane, and to look for a job.

A recruiting agency set me up for three days of interviews up and down the Gulf coast, and on the third day I walked out of an elegant New Orleans practice with an unsigned contract in hand. I made my way out of the city and after crossing Lake Ponchartrain slipped off Interstate 10 for the scenic route back to Biloxi. It was about seventy-five miles from Jane's apartment to New Orleans, and I wondered as I drove through one small bayou settlement after another whether I would ever get to see Jane with such a long commute. I stopped at a seafood shack for a late lunch and while eating a fried shrimp po' boy eyed an unhygienic-appearing urgent care center across the street. I didn't see any help wanted signs in the window but decided that there was no harm in asking. The doctor, a gruff older man with a Burl Ives beard and belly, looked at my references, pronounced me overqualified for his clinic, and predicted that I would abandon the state within three months, girlfriend or no girlfriend.

As I was leaving, the doctor added, seemingly as an afterthought, "One place that might not bore you too much is the health center up on Frederick Douglas. They haven't had a real doctor up there for years."

"Thanks," I said. "Do you think I'd last there more than three months?"

"If you do," he replied with a grin, "you'd be the first."

Once I found Frederick Douglas Boulevard, the clinic, a square concrete bunker set in a neighborhood of tar paper-roofed plywood shacks, was not hard to spot. A peeling coat of light blue paint attempted in vain to give the building a cheerful demeanor. I parked in back and followed the windowless walls to the front door. It was pleasant to step out of the blazing late afternoon sun into the cool fluorescent dimness.

"I sure am sorry, but we're not seeing drug reps today," said the receptionist.

Suddenly feeling sheepish about my uninvited visit, I handed her my references and mumbled, "Actually, I'm a doctor. I was just wondering if you could use an internist here."

The receptionist raised her eyebrows and with a bright smile replied, "We sure could! Let me tell the medical director that you're here."

The waiting room was quiet but crowded, and I squeezed into a plastic orange chair between a big-boned woman and a bright-eyed child. The woman stared straight ahead, both of us pretending not to notice the way her large frame spilled onto my right leg and shoulder, but the child beamed at me with a megawatt smile and sent me off to my interview with a high-pitched giggle.

"Come on in," said the medical director. "I'm Lamar Blackwell." I accepted his invitation and for the second time in the last ten minutes had to adjust my eyes to a dimming of the lights. Stepping into Lamar's tiny hole in the wall, illuminated only by a small fluorescent desk lamp, was like entering a poorly lit cave. Stack upon stack of medical charts rose from the floor like stalagmites and added to the office's cave-like feeling.

Lamar, who had a disheveled post-call look that I recognized all too well, scanned my references and said, "They didn't tell me they were sending someone down, but good. It's about time."

"Pardon me," I said, "but I'm not sure which 'they' you're referring to."

"The Public Health Service, of course," he replied, his blood-shot eyes peering at me quizzically. "Aren't you here to do your time?"

It dawned on me that Lamar thought I'd been sent by the government to pay back a Public Health Service scholarship. "No, I'm just here because the Air Force assigned my girlfriend to Keesler for the next three years," I explained, then added quickly, "Not that there aren't many other fine reasons to settle down in the area."

Lamar started to laugh but let it wind down to a weary yawn. "Here's the deal," he said. "I'm an obstetrician, Clay Cooper's our pediatrician, and Barbara Morgan's our nurse practitioner.

We haven't had an internist for three years. You'll share call every other night and every other weekend with Barry Smith, a family practitioner up the road a ways, who'll be thrilled because he's been on call every night and every weekend for as long as I can remember. I'll have to check your references, of course, and run your name by the Board of Directors, but that should be a formality. The sooner you start, the better, and here's what I can offer you." He wrote a figure on a piece of paper and showed it to me.

Lamar's offer was short one zero compared with the one in my pocket. As I stared at the numbers on the page, they blurred into grainy images of the fine old gentleman-doctor who had offered me a job earlier in the day and the view of the quaint New Orleans street from what would be my window in the stately brick building. Lamar's eyes drooped shut, and he started to snore. The long line of teenage mothers-to-be in the hallway squirmed restlessly as I sat in the semi-darkness of Lamar's office, rewinding in my mind the long journey between Jane's apartment and New Orleans; I would be able to get home from the clinic in less time than it would take just to cross the Lake Ponchartrain Bridge. To heck with the missing zero, I decided. Lamar seemed pleased with my decision, once he managed to wake up and wipe the drool off his chin.

"You're going where, to do what?" my fellow residents exclaimed when I returned to Boston, though the ones who knew Jane nodded approvingly.

"You're on your own now," the Chief of Medicine warned me on our final day. "Don't embarrass the program." The Chief's farewell reminded me that I was no longer a cocky resident backed by a deep medical staff but a clueless rookie doctor. I promised not to hold the Chief accountable for all the mistakes I was about to make and drove off to begin my medical career.

Jane and I had eased into the South the previous year, Jane's over-packed hatchback revving bravely through the high passes in the Blue Ridge and Smoky Mountains before coasting onto the flatlands of southeastern Tennessee and Alabama. We strolled on the hillsides of Monticello, tasted our first grits in Roanoke, heard our first "y'all" in Cherokee, took each other's pictures outside Dollywood, got wrapped in our first wet-blanket Southern haze in Knoxville, had our first fried catfish dinner in Meridien, caught our first glimpse of the Gulf of Mexico in Gulfport, and arrived at the base in Biloxi just in time for Jane to begin her tour of duty as an Air Force pediatrics resident.

This time, though, I stayed on the superhighways, my Mustang slicing through the increasingly thick Southern air as I made my way from Denny's to Denny's and Circle 8 to Circle 8. My only sightseeing stop was at Fulton County Stadium in Atlanta, where I hoped to see one of my favorite baseball players, the great Dale Murphy. Right field was being patrolled that night, however, by a rookie named Dave Justice.

"Where's Dale Murphy?" I asked the person next to me.

He seemed startled by my ignorance of current events, then appeared to gather from my accent and the crisp newness of my Braves cap that I must be an out-of-towner. "The Braves traded Murph yesterday," he informed me. "The whole city's in mourning."

My timing was better the next evening, as I pulled into Jane's apartment complex just as she was returning from a two-week training exercise in combat casualty care in the deserts of southern Texas. Jane's timing, too, was impeccable in its own way. Saddam Hussein had invaded Kuwait while Jane was in Texas carrying mock-wounded Marines on makeshift litters and crossing dry creek beds on rope ladders, and, having passed her course, Jane was now a good candidate to ship out to Saudi Arabia and the yet-to-be-named Operation Desert Shield. But the problems of the world seemed far away at that moment, and as we crossed the parking lot toward each other, it mattered not that Jane's fatigues were begrimed with Texas dust and sweat and that she was encased in bug spray; we were together again, and nothing else seemed to matter.

I drove along Frederick Douglas Boulevard slowly on my first day of work, my windows down and the air-conditioning off in spite of the blistering heat; I wanted to see, hear, and smell the neighborhood without a panel of tinted glass in the way. In the heavy breezeless air there was neither the rustle of leaves to mask the sound of chickens scratching in the dirt nor any wafting away of the smell of manure in the tiny gardens, and the neighbors stared at me from their cinder block stoops with languid curiosity as I cruised slowly down the street.

Sandy, the secretary who had mistaken me for a pharmaceutical rep, greeted me at the door of the clinic. "Welcome to Gulf Coast Family Health," she said with the same bright smile. "I've got some good news and some bad news for you."

"I'll take the bad news first," I replied.

"The bad news is that you've just inherited 3,000 new patients," Sandy said.

"And the good news?" I asked.

"That only half of them need to see you today," she replied.

"I'll bet you say that every time a new internist arrives," I joked.

Sandy tilted her head and thought for a moment. "Well, that's been the problem," she said. "None of us can remember the last time that happened."

Nan, my peppery medical assistant, showed me my office and examining room. I pointed at a poster on the examining room wall which depicted a cross-eyed mutt sitting in a bucket of soap suds. The caption read, "Dirt is Mother Nature's way of reminding you to take a bath."

"Please take that down, Nan," I said. "It's insulting."

"Mm-hmm," Nan agreed with an amused shake of her head that I would come to recognize very well.

My two minute orientation completed, I rolled up my sleeves and tossed my stethoscope around my neck and by mid-morning had arrived at two sobering conclusions: that Sandy's prediction had barely been an exaggeration and that in seven years of medical school and residency I had never really seen diabetes. I had helped take care of diabetic patients and thought I understood the ravages of the disease, but I wasn't prepared to hear the Velcro-like sound of a grime-hardened sock peeling off a deep oozing foot ulcer or to feel the withered lifelessness of a gangrenous toe. Nor was I prepared to respond to a finger-stick blood sugar reading in the 400's or come up with a treatment plan for a blind, edematous patient in severe heart and kidney failure who seemed to have no business being alive. Prepared or not, though, I was the one who had to make the decisions now, and so I did, patient by patient and problem by problem, until that first morning finally ended and by some miracle neither the patients nor I had keeled over, at least not yet.

Clay Cooper, the pediatrician, dropped by my office with a bagged lunch. He was clearly amused by my shell-shocked appearance. "You'll get used to it," he reassured me through giant mouthfuls of peanut butter and jelly. "The main thing you have to learn is to adjust your expectations. Forget about micro-managing blood sugars and hitting blood pressure targets. Just keeping these people alive is an accomplishment, so don't feel bad if they go through some serious s--- along the way."

"Thanks for the advice," I said. "So, how long have you been working here?"

"Oh, a little while," Clay replied vaguely. He washed down the last bite of his sandwich with three gulps of Dr. Pepper and squirmed a bit uneasily. "I had to move out-of-state to get away from my ex-wife's blood-sucking lawyers. Left a darn good practice back in Oklahoma. I'll tell you what, though. Working here is the purest form of medicine I've ever practiced. We're less motivated by money, do more good work with fewer resources, and take care of sicker people than most doctors. What we're doing is special, and you should feel proud to work here." He sat back with a small but satisfying belch and nodded, the picture of altruistic contentment.

Lucia, the pediatric medical assistant, poked her head through one of my doorways. "Dr. Cooper," she complained, "we be out of those loopy ear wax removal thingies."

Clay leaped out of his chair and threw his arms into the air, his empty can of Dr. Pepper inadvertently flying out of his hand and sailing just past Lucia's nose. "Why the hell am I wasting my time in a dump like this?" he shouted. He stormed out of the room, leaving me to roll up his sandwich wrapper and brown bag and toss them in the trash.

My run on diabetic patients seemed over until the middle of the afternoon, when a tall, gaunt man staggered into my office and collapsed onto the floor. "I'm sorry," panted Melanie, the receptionist who came running in after him. "I told him he couldn't just barge in here. This is Jesse Carter, the town drunk."

"Not…drunk…don't…drink," gasped Jesse before passing out.

"Oh, he drinks all right," commented Melanie. "We see him stumbling drunk around this neighborhood all the time. Do you need some help?"

I knelt beside Jesse and examined him quickly. He was unresponsive to voice and his pulse was weak, but he was breathing.

"Please ask Nan to bring the glucometer," I said to Melanie.

A minute later, while I was listening to Jesse's heart and lungs and getting ready to check his blood pressure, Nan announced, "His blood sugar is sixteen."

I have never been confident about starting intravenous lines, and as Nan wheeled the crash cart into my office and stood by with an ampule of D50 I contemplated the humiliation of having a patient die right in front of me on my first day of work because I couldn't start a line. If that happened, I would have to leave and never return, and it occurred to me that the urgent care doctor's prediction of my three-month demise would have been generously long by eighty-nine days. But blood back-flashed into the catheter, and as I pushed the D50 into Jesse's glucose-depleted veins his nearly inanimate eyelids fluttered back to life.

"I'm not a drunk," were Jesse's first words after his wits had been revived by the infusion of sugar.

"I can see that," I said. "You just had a hypoglycemic reaction. How much insulin do you take? And what have you had to eat today?"

"Can't say exactly how much insulin," Jesse replied weakly. "Half a syringe, sometimes more maybe. And as far as eating, well there's been more days than not lately where I haven't had nothing to eat at all. I still takes my insulin, though, when I can get it. Last doc said I needs it for my diabetes."

I admonished Jesse about the dangers of taking insulin without any food and advised him to skip his medicine on his hungry days. Melanie so regretted accusing Jesse of being a drunk when he had actually been staggering around town in an insulin-induced fog that she insisted on buying him some groceries.

Most of the time, though, our diabetic patients suffered from hyperglycemia rather than hypoglycemia. They were welcome to visit any morning to get their blood sugars checked, and a bubbly young woman named Diane Johnson took advantage of that offer quite often during my first few weeks at the clinic. I was impressed by Diane's interest in her glucose levels, which hovered insistently around 400 in spite of the precipitous manner in which we climbed her insulin dosage ladder, but Nan laughed when I complimented Diane's good intentions. "A lot of the ladies just like Pam to do their finger sticks," she said. "It takes the place of getting their nails done, which they can't afford." Whatever the reason for Diane's visits, I finally had to respond when her fasting blood sugar climbed into the 500's in spite of being on a cumulative daily dose of almost 300 units of insulin.

Diane looked a little sweaty and shaky but was otherwise her usual cheerful self when I told her I was admitting her to the hospital. "I don't get why my sugars are so high," she said. "I eats like a bird. Just some jelly sandwiches now and then."

I wrote admitting orders for nutritional counseling and sliding scale coverage of her blood sugars and over the next few days was pleased to see her glucose levels trend into the low 100's with single digit doses of short-acting insulin before meals and a modest amount of long-acting insulin at bedtime. I walked into Diane's room on her fourth afternoon in the hospital with the satisfied glow of a missionary who has converted an entire heathen village to Christianity. "You're doing great," I purred. "See how little insulin you need with the right diet? I'll send you home tomorrow if your sugar is still this good."

I couldn't find Diane on the floor the next morning. I did find her chart, however, which showed that her sugars had climbed back into the 400's overnight. "Your patient's been wandering," one of the nurses informed me.

"Where?" I asked.

"To the cafeteria," the nurse chuckled. "You might want to keep her in restraints next time."

I found Diane at one end of a long cafeteria table, just a few seats down from a trio of beefy urologists who seemed amazed and amused in equal measure by the gravy-slathered mountain of eggs, sausages, grits, toast, and pastries on Diane's tray and the degree to which it dwarfed their own not insubstantial pre-OR breakfasts. "They weren't feeding me upstairs," Diane said with a shrug. "Just those itty-bitty fruit and vegetable plates and things like that. So I came down last night for a real supper, and now I want a little breakfast before you send me away."

"I know diabetic meals can leave you a little unsatisfied," I conceded, "but don't you think that two or maybe even one of those Danishes would have been enough for breakfast?"

"Like I told you, Doctor, I eats like a bird when I'm at home," Diane insisted.

"A large carnivorous bird of prey, maybe," I muttered as I headed back upstairs to write her discharge orders and finish my rounds.

The nurses enjoyed a good laugh when I returned to the floor, and I laughed with them, even though I knew they were gently making fun of me, the naive rookie doctor who thought he and his clever insulin scale had gotten his nutritionally wayward patient to see the light after a lifetime of bad eating habits. I knew they would admonish Diane in an equally gentle manner when she returned from the cafeteria. These nurses had introduced me to Southern manners; their laughter, easily offered and free of malice and mockery, had helped ease the jitters of my first few days of hospital rounds, and I found myself trying to emulate the nonjudgmental way in which they treated even the poorest and least compliant of patients.

I discovered that the medical staff, though more reserved in manner than the nursing staff, was keeping an eye out for me as well. A net-casting fisherman named Earl Crosby struggled into my office late one afternoon complaining of excruciating low back pain. Earl's pain had started abruptly while loading his sinker-weighted nets and a hefty haul of fish and crabs onto the back of his truck, and it seemed likely that he had simply strained his lower back. The most notable aspect of Earl's physical exam, apart from his obvious extreme discomfort, was some weakness in his right ankle, suggesting the added possibility of a herniated lumbar disc, an unfortunate but not unexpected consequence of a lifetime of heavy lifting. I sent Earl to the hospital with admitting orders for lab tests, pain medications as needed throughout the night, and a CT scan of his spine in the morning.

The floor nurse called me during the 10:00 nightly news with lab results; they were notable for an elevated BUN and creatinine, indicating that Earl's kidneys were not functioning properly. I had no idea how well his kidneys usually functioned and told her we would do some more studies in the morning. The nurse woke me up a few hours later to report that Earl's blood pressure had dropped, that he was unconscious, and that his feet were cold and blue. It took a few seconds for my still-sleeping brain to process the new information, but then the probable cause of Earl's back pain became clear: an abdominal aortic aneurysm that had dissected through his renal arteries and then ruptured. I told the nurse that I would be right there and asked her in the meanwhile to see if there was a bed free in the ICU.

The sickening feeling of adrenaline overdose, all too familiar from sprinting to countless Code 99's during my internship and residency, accompanied me as I pushed my Mustang through the humid night, grateful for the lane reflectors which guided my bulging yet bleary eyes all the way to the hospital. It was my fourth week on the job and my first middle of the night hospital crisis, and as I screeched into the nearly empty doctors' parking lot and ran up the stairs to the medical floor, I realized that once I reached Earl's bedside I wouldn't be sure what to do next.

The floor nurse waved me off when she saw me race-walking down the hall. "Mr. Crosby just got to the ICU," she called out. "Good luck."

I spun around and ran down the stairs to the ICU, astonished at how quickly Earl had been transferred. I was even more surprised when I walked into the ICU and saw Tom Moore, one of the emergency room doctors, at Earl's bedside along with Howard Thurmond, our nephrologist, and Bob Harmon, one of our surgeons. "The ER docs cover the night-time codes," Tom explained, "and even though this wasn't a code the nurse asked me to help out, seeing as you're new around here. When she told me you suspected a dissecting aneurysm and that his kidneys had shut down I figured we could use Howard's and Bob's help, too. I hope you don't mind that we're all here."

My knees almost buckled, so precipitously did the mere presence of colleagues drop my adrenaline levels. I leaned as casually as I could against Earl's bedside table, put my hands in my pockets so no one could see how much they were shaking, and said, "Not at all. I appreciate your help."

Tom excused himself and returned to the emergency room. Howard and Bob, both appearing 3:00 AM-rumpled but alert, observed patiently as I did my bedside exam, which revealed that poor Earl was hypotensive, unresponsive, and pulseless below the waist, while a quick glance at the collecting bag for his Foley catheter, which had been inserted by the floor nurse, revealed that he had stopped making urine.

"Well, what do you think?" Howard asked.

It did indeed look like a massive aortic dissection, I replied, adding that Earl already seemed to be beyond our help. Howard and Bob agreed and, sensing my feelings of guilt, reassured me that a catastrophic event like this couldn't have been foreseen or prevented. They also concurred that surgery was out of the question. "He'd die on the table," Bob stated emphatically. "I wouldn't touch him." Howard and Bob left me to my bedside vigil but reappeared when the Crosby clan arrived, helping me explain why nothing could be done for their patriarch. Earl, mercifully, didn't linger long, and dawn was just breaking as I put a sympathetic hand on the shoulder of the newly widowed Mrs. Crosby and went off to start my morning rounds.

As I made my way through the halls, exhausted and discouraged, one doctor after another, many of whom I hadn't even met, nodded to me and said, "Good job." I didn't know what was going on until Glen Hamilton, the Chief of Staff and one of our ear, nose, and throat surgeons, pulled me aside and explained, "Howard Thurmond has been spreading the word that you handled a tough case real well last night."

"What's he talking about?" I replied. "I missed the diagnosis, and the guy died right in front of me."

Glen shook his head. "Catastrophes happen. It wasn't your fault. Howard said you hung in there with your patient, and that means something to us."

I continued my rounds, a bit miffed at first to think that Howard and Bob had come during the night as much to evaluate me as to assist me. Then my sleep-deprived brain began to comprehend how much the approval of these old-time Mississippi doctors meant to me, and even though I knew that the raw memories of Earl's final hours would flash unbidden into my thoughts for years to come, my step as I finished rounds had a renewed bounce, one which had nothing to do with the cups of black coffee which I chugged at the nurses' station.

Mornings at the hospital always took longer than expected. Even on the rare occasions when I got through rounds efficiently, someone from medical records would flag me down to sign an old telephone order, or one of the family practitioners would pull me aside for a curbside consult. And I almost never left the hospital without saying hello to the medical staff secretary, whose Chelsea childhood and Mississippi marriage had produced a peculiar brew of Boston "aah's" and Southern "y'alls" and who always sent me off with a "Go Sox!" farewell. I would then jump in my car and dash to the clinic, hoping as I snuck through the back door for just one quiet and unnoticed moment at my desk before starting the rest of my day.

Those hopes evaporated in memorable fashion one morning when virtually the entire staff rushed to greet me at the back door when they heard it creak open. So many of them started talking at once, and in such breathless fashion, that it took me a minute to grasp that Rosie Jordan was having a seizure in the waiting room.

My first visit with Rosie, back during my earliest days at the clinic, had started as a long, awkward monologue. Rosie didn't respond when I introduced myself, glared at me from under her heavy brow when I tried to elicit a chief complaint, and hunkered down in wary silence on the examining table as I attempted to make sense of her thick, illegible, and ultimately useless medical chart. "I think this note from seven years ago says that you were to start some high blood pressure medications," I said. "Do you take any now?" No answer. "According to your chart," I tried again, "your blood sugar runs a little on the high side. Do you try to follow a diabetic diet?" There was no answer to that question, either, or to the one after that.

"All right, Rosie," I finally conceded, "for our first visit I'll just check your blood pressure, okay?" Rosie sat so rigidly, her plump arms pulled tightly against her massive torso, that I had difficulty prying an arm loose for the blood pressure check, and she appeared not to have moved a muscle when I returned a few minutes later with a bottle of antihypertensive medication.

"Is that all?" Rosie lisped. When I nodded, she gave me a smile so warm and broad that her eyes practically disappeared into her fleshy cheeks. "I was so afraid that you was going to be mean!"

"I'm never mean, Rosie," I reassured her. "Dumb, sometimes, but never mean. Take one of these twice per day and come back in two weeks, okay?"

Rosie was back in two days. She had forgotten to take her pills, but she had taken the time to knit me a doily that appeared either off-white or slightly soiled, depending on the lighting. "For your coffee cup," read the attached note, "from Your Little Cockroach."

"I'm touched," I told Rosie. "And it would make me feel even better if you took your pills."

Rosie nodded with another one of her crinkly-eyed smiles and departed without a word. She was back a few days later with a stained, gimp-laced vinyl change purse, a few days after that with a faded post card of the Smoky Mountains, and so on until I had a drawer full of Rosie's little Boo Radley-like treasures, each delivered with a note of explanation from "Your Little Cockroach", a

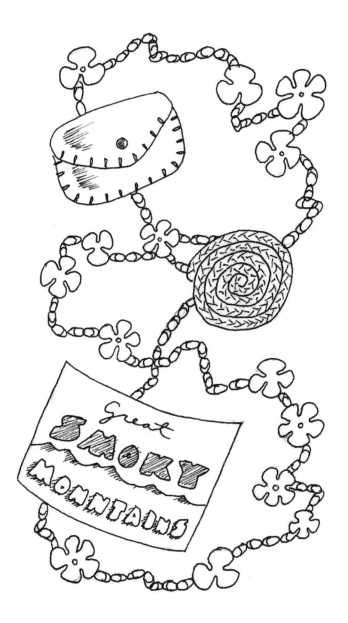

nickname which seemed more incongruous every time I examined her 350-plus pound frame. With each visit I pieced together a bit more of Rosie's complex medical picture, and by the time she brought me a lei made of plastic flowers and paper clips, I felt that we had her on a medication regimen which addressed her major issues, even though I was unable to identify the syndrome which in all likelihood unified her unusual constellation of physical and metabolic anomalies.

Rosie's visits stopped as abruptly as they had begun. "She's always been like that," Nan shrugged when I inquired about Rosie's sudden absence. "Comes and goes, goes and comes. Likes your attention, though, Rosie does, mm-hmm. Don't worry, she'll be back."

She's back all right, I thought as I ran to the waiting room with my entourage of over -excited secretaries and medical assistants. I had taken care of patients with grand-mal seizures as a resident but never outside the well-supported setting of an emergency room or an intensive care unit. Seizure management protocols raced through my mind alongside old doubts about my ability to start an emergency IV line. I realized with a rush of panic and regret that I hadn't taken the time to learn what anti-seizure medications we had in the crash cart.

The chair over which Rosie was sprawled was so obscured by her bulk that Rosie appeared for one improbable moment to be suspended in mid-air like a gigantic marionette. She was sitting by herself, the rest of the patients in the waiting area having fled to the other side of the room. Rosie glanced at me as I approached and sporadically flung her arms and legs in random directions. As I came closer she closed her eyes and let loose a few head and body shivers. I breathed a grateful sigh of relief; Rosie was not having a seizure but was simply flailing her limbs, probably to get some attention. I let my heart rate decelerate, knelt in front of Rosie, and took her by the hand. "Rosie," I said, "open your eyes and look at me. Come on now, open your eyes and look at me. I know you can do it. There, that's good. Now I want you to stop shaking. That's it, that's the way. Stop shaking. Slowly now, slowly…Good job, Rosie, good job. Well done."

Rosie smiled at me and said, "Hi Doc. Your little cockroach is back."

"All right, Rosie," I replied, "come on back to the examining room so I can finish checking you out."

After helping Rosie to her feet I turned around to face twenty widely gaping mouths and forty even more widely gaping eyes (or thirty-nine, rather, considering that old Mr. Amos Jefferson had one glass eye).

"Dang, he's good," I heard someone say.

We were noticeably busier over the next week. I attributed the increase in visits to random variation, but Nan informed me that the story of Rosie's "seizure" had spread around the neighborhood, accompanied by the exciting rumor that the clinic had hired a healer. I was stricken by an appalling Biblical vision of an endless line of miracle-seeking patients - lepers, the possessed, and even the deceased among them. "Nan," I pleaded, "you've got to get the word out that Rosie wasn't even having a seizure!"

"Mm-hmm," Nan replied in her uniquely ambiguous fashion, agreeing with me verbally while at the same time dismissing me with an amused shake of her head. "Like they'll all believe that!" In spite of Nan's skepticism, the rumors of my healing powers faded almost as quickly as they had begun, though I did continue to be identified every now and then as "the doctor who cured Rosie of her seizures".

I thought wistfully about Rosie's miraculous "cure" as I sat in Barbara's office, looking from Luanne to Larry and then back to Luanne and pondering what a long and difficult road lay ahead of them. Nobody, I realized, would ever identify me as the person who cured Larry of his HIV. At first glance Larry and Luanne didn't look like brother and sister; Luanne was heading toward round-cheeked stoutness, while Larry was long-limbed and lanky. A second glance, however, showed that they shared the same warm brown eyes and gentle demeanor, though Luanne's steady gaze also held a tinge of wariness. "Doctor, can you help my brother?" she asked again.

Luanne's question snapped me out of my distracted musings. "Yes, I can help," I replied. "It's serious business, though. What do you know about HIV, Larry?"

Larry looked at the floor. "It's a virus that got into my blood during my operation," he mumbled uncomfortably. Then he looked up, his discomfort suddenly displaced by child-like curiosity. "Hey Doc," he asked, "when someone has HIV how come you don't just take out all their blood and replace it with clean blood?"

"Unfortunately, the virus doesn't just get into the blood stream but into other body tissues as well," I replied. "So I'm afraid that even if we replaced all your blood, we wouldn't be able to get rid of all of the virus."

"Oh," Larry said. He cast his eyes downward once again, and I kicked myself not only for my coldly clinical answer but also for having substituted "your blood" for "their blood", thus breaking the momentary illusion that we might have been talking about someone else.

Larry and I moved next door for his physical exam. He was even thinner than he first appeared, and the scars from his gunshot wounds and surgical incisions felt gnarled and knotty when I palpated his abdomen. "Does your belly still hurt?" I asked.

"Not really," Larry said, "except in my memories. Hey, Doc?"

"Yes?"

"Does it hurt a lot? AIDS, I mean."

"No, AIDS doesn't hurt. Mostly you feel tired, and once in a while you might feel kind of sick. But it doesn't hurt."

Larry nodded thoughtfully. "Yeah, I been a little tired," he admitted, then asked unexpectedly, "Do you like roundball, Doc?"

"If you mean basketball, then yes, I do. How about you?"

"Yeah, I play some. I like to watch, too. Who's your favorite player?"

"I'm from Boston, so I'm a big Larry Bird fan."

"Bird is good," Larry agreed. "But Magic Johnson's better. He's my guy. I learned how to pass from watching him. See, I've got my Magic Johnson sneakers on." Larry held up for my inspection a well-worn but still expensive-looking basketball shoe. He had big feet - size twelve, I guessed.

We rejoined Luanne in Barbara's office. "Larry looks fine," I said. "He should get some blood tests today, and we'll meet in a week to go over the results." Luanne's stare remained impassive, but I knew what she was thinking: that the results weren't going to be good, and that I was just a useless doctor who wouldn't be able to save her little brother.

Sam, our file room clerk, shuffled into my office the following Monday and dropped a piece of paper on my desk. "Sorry, Doc, found another one!" he apologized in his customary manner. Lucky Sam, I thought as I stared at Larry's lab report, wishing that I too were unable to comprehend the dreadful story contained within those cryptic rows of letters and numbers.

"Hey Doc," said Larry. He and Luanne were seated right below my poster of the bubble-bathing cross-eyed mutt (which Nan had discreetly re-hung one particularly aromatic afternoon, followed on my part by an equally discreet lack of protest). Larry was in the same baggy sweat suit he'd been wearing the previous week; I couldn't tell if he had lost weight or if my eyes were being influenced by the numbers on his lab report.

"Hello," I replied. "How are you guys doing?"

Luanne ignored my pleasantries. "How are the test results?" she asked.

I cleared my throat, ready to expound on the differences between T4 and T8 cells, being HIV positive and having AIDS, and routine and opportunistic infections. As Larry and Luanne locked their eyes on me, though, their expressions hovering between trust and fear, I decided to abandon the lecture I had been preparing for the last three days.

"The numbers don't look great, Larry," I said. "The counts on your helper cells have gone down, to the point where we now have to say that you've got AIDS."

Luanne sobbed once, then composed herself and patted her brother on the hand. "So Doc," asked Larry, "how long am I gonna live?"

"Nobody can predict these things, Larry," I replied evasively. "Listen, I want you to start taking some medications. Some you take every day, some you take once or twice a week. Unfortunately, all these medications can make you feel a little sick. They're the best we've got, though, and there's a good chance that they won't bother you too much."

I took out my prescription pad and started to scribble one polysyllabic drug name after another, each accompanied by a coded set of instructions about milligrams and dosing intervals. The familiar act of writing the prescriptions had a calming effect on me, and for a moment, but just a fleeting one, our plan, captured neatly and scientifically on an official-looking stack of papers, seemed like it might actually work.

"When should we meet again, Doctor?" Luanne asked.

I looked at my calendar, a freebie from our local Chevrolet dealer. Bubba Belliveau's smiling face filled most of the page and loomed over the days, weeks, and months tucked like an afterthought into the bottom right-hand corner. Bubba made a year look awfully short. "Next week, same time," I said. "In fact, let's plan on meeting every Thursday at one. I want to keep track of how you're doing."

Larry did show up every Thursday afternoon that fall, one of several patients who we locked into regular weekly time slots: on Mondays I expected Thelma Nixon, whose pulmonary sarcoidosis left her alarmingly short of breath; Tuesdays were the day for Hulbert Bailey, another heavy breather, though in his case from a lifetime of inhaling cigarette smoke and bad air at the shrimp processing factory (the aroma of which, unfortunately, he always brought with him); on Wednesdays I visited with Molly McNair, a cheerful asthmatic whose steroid-induced round cheeks gave her head a nearly perfect spherical shape. Rosie Jordan no longer came to see me on a weekly basis, though she did for some time page me almost every night that I was on call to say, "Doctor, I's tryin' to have a seizure!"; I would advise Rosie to try not to have a seizure and then attempt, usually in vain, to go back to sleep. There were other regulars, too, but I found myself looking forward most to Larry's visits. He tended to sit quietly except for the times that we talked about basketball. "Hey Doc, you ever see Larry Bird play?" he asked one afternoon. Sure, I answered, and told him about some of the other great basketball players that I'd had a chance to see, such as Pete Maravich, Michael Jordan, John Havlicek, George Gervin, and Bernard King, not to mention Larry's favorite, Magic Johnson, who I saw once at the Forum in Los Angeles. I also told Larry about going with my father and brother to my first Celtics game, of which my most vivid memory was Bill Russell intercepting a pass, outracing the entire Baltimore Bullets team down the length of the court, and finishing the play with an emphatic dunk.

"Nice," said Larry. "I'll bet my dad would take me to a game, too, if I ever find him. Hey, Doc, did I ever tell you I was looking for my dad when I got shot?" I shook my head, and he continued. "I asked Luanne a couple of years ago if she knew where our dad was, and she said she'd heard he might be in Memphis. So I caught a ride up there, thought I might find him. One day I was playing roundball with some of the neighborhood kids, and some other kids drove by and shot us. I don't remember much after that, except for Luanne coming to bring me home."

Larry didn't show up the following Thursday or the Thursday after that. He and Luanne didn't have a telephone, but Nan tracked Luanne down somehow and found out that Larry had disappeared. Luanne said he had probably gone back to Memphis to look for his father. Larry had mumbled something about his father one day, the first time he had done so since being shot, and the next day he was gone. I suspected that our conversation had put this idea in his head, but Nan told me not to feel guilty. "Sixteen might seem young to you," she said, "but around here that's a man, and a man makes his own decisions."

I had the secretaries keep Larry's regular time slot open, but it remained unfilled as we moved past Thanksgiving and into the Christmas season. The summer heat had finally broken at the beginning of November; while driving along the shore on our first crisp fall morning, I had been startled by the sight of an enormous container crane, a mere six blocks from the hospital but previously invisible in the soup-like summer haze. Even with the break in the heat, there was still but the barest nip of coldness in the air. While the balmy temperatures made it seem less like Christmas to me, the legions of snowmen and reindeer on our neighbors' lawns seemed to feel otherwise. Holiday spirits ran high at the clinic, too, where my co-workers wished me Merry Christmas so often that I came close to blurting "Bah humbug!" on several occasions. Even Mr. Leroy, our whistling custodian, changed the tune to which he marched with his trusty push-broom, cycling endlessly through the first four bars of "Deck the Halls", never to achieve any sort of melodic resolution.

The clinic staff was so determined to get me to the Christmas Eve luncheon that I would have suspected mischief had I not chalked up their determination to Southern hospitality. I arrived at the party a little bit late and was ushered to a seat in front of a huge platter of steamed crawfish. "All we've ever seen you eat are the turkey sandwiches and apples that you bring for lunch every day," explained Loretta Dean, one of the nurses, with a mischievous grin. "We want to see if a New Englander can handle some real food."

"But it's Christmas!" I said. "Shouldn't we be eating honey-baked ham and roasted chestnuts and stuff like that?"

"Forget it," replied Loretta. "This is Christmas in Mississippi!"

Quite a crowd gathered to see if I could eat like a true Southerner. What they didn't realize was that while growing up I had partaken of many a family meal in Boston's Chinatown, where apart from pickled jellied quails' eggs I had learned to swallow, if not necessarily relish, all manner of exotic fauna. And so it was without fear that I twisted the heads off the poor little crustaceans, sucked the spiced steamed meat out of their bodies, scooped out their brains with my right little finger, and slurped it all down with swigs of sweet Southern tea. The staff applauded when I tossed aside my last empty shell and rose to take a bow.

At one point I would have been surprised that people could be entertained by watching me eat crawfish, but I had come to learn how seriously my co-workers practiced the fine art of enjoying a meal. We had pot-luck lunches one Friday each month, and while I never got over my old medical school habit of wolfing down a plateful of food and rushing back to work, I did during those brief interludes observe how much my co-workers appreciated life's little pleasures, such as the ritual of enjoying Sandy's biscuits.

"Mmm, mmm, mmm," Sam would invariably say after a few slow and rapturous sniffs. "Miss Sandy, your biscuits are calling out to me by name!"

"She makes them so light and flaky," Pam, our lab technician, would add with a shake of her head. "All these years, and she won't tell me her secret."

"I can never decide which way I like Miss Sandy's biscuits best," was Mr. Leroy's predictable contribution. "Plain, with just a touch of melting butter, or with a spoonful of Miss Melanie's sweet gravy." And on it would go, with the conversation now shifting to the rich flavor and creamy texture of Melanie's gravy.

Some Christmas caroling and gift exchanges broke out after I cleared my crawfish platter, until Lamar Blackwell held up his hands for silence and began to speak, slowly at first and then with growing passion, about the sacred mission on which we were all embarked as health care workers for the poor. With eyes closed, head thrown back, arms raised to the heavens, and voice quavering with emotion, Lamar looked much more like a tent evangelist than an obstetrician. "Yes, sir!" people would shout in response to some of Lamar's more stirring exhortations. The crowd was moved to form a large circle - whether spontaneously or from practiced custom I couldn't tell - and when Lamar finished speaking, we joined hands and ended the party with a chorus of, "Did I ever tell you you're my hero? You are the wind beneath my wings."

I cruised slowly through the December dusk, my path along the shore guided by the twinkling Christmas lights in the antebellum houses to my right and the blinking safety lights on the homebound fishing boats to my left. I picked up Jane, who had been working since the previous morning, at the base hospital, and we spent our first Christmas Eve together lying on the sofa, drifting in and out of sleep while one Christmas movie after another played on cable television. An occasional familiar line would penetrate our consciousness, such as "The only miracle I want to see tonight is your daddy walking through that door" and "The spirits did it all in one night - but of course they can, they're spirits!". For the most part, though, we just dozed inside our drowsy little cocoon until midnight, when I turned off the television and woke up Jane to wish her a Merry Christmas. "I'm sorry," she murmured, "that I kept you from going home for Christmas."

"I am home," I replied. I don't think Jane heard me. She had fallen back to sleep.

A chill winter wind finally blew into the region after the New Year, just as the rest of the world was reaching an historic boiling point. Jane was working the night that Operation Desert Shield turned into Operation Desert Storm, and the bombs started falling on Baghdad as I was on my way to the base with Jane's supper. The MP at the gate, spotting the captain's decal on my car window, waved me through with a crisp salute, and I tried to snap off a good patriotic salute in return, though it ended up as a barely improved version of my usual sheepish half-wave. I drove to the hospital along the flight line road, picturesque as always as it wound along the bayou shore, but now I saw menace in the murky silhouettes of the warplanes, hulking shadows against the inky sky. Over the tense weeks which followed, I sometimes pulled my car to the side of the road to watch the steady stream of takeoffs and landings from the base. The fighter jets, which after screaming overhead would disappear into the clear blue sky in an impossibly short period of time, were the most impressive aircraft. I was more transfixed, though, by the transport planes; the slow motion ascent of their ungainly bodies over the mottled surface of the bayou was almost comical, but it made me shudder to imagine Jane being borne by one of them to the war or to some other faraway base.

The winter chill was brief, though, and a quick thaw allowed me to experience January fishing for the first time. Loretta Dean, hearing that Jane was on call Super Bowl Sunday, invited me to her home to watch the game and enjoy a fresh catfish dinner. Loretta's husband, Clifford, who worked for the state but did some farming on the side, had dug a couple of ponds between his back yard and his corn field and stocked one pond with bass and the other with catfish. We put a couple of fishing rods in the back of Clifford's pickup truck and made the short drive to the ponds from Clifford and Loretta's cozy bungalow. A burly, bearded fellow who always seemed a bit winded, Clifford kept up a cordial though breathless stream of chatter as we fished and seemed to enjoy providing a play by play narrative of his every cast. "I'm cinching this knot...good old clinch knot, see... like this," he would huff and puff, "then cast it right there...dug that spot a bit

deeper, see…because I know it makes a good spot…for the bass to hang out…now I'm retrieving…my spoon lure…Nothing that time…we'll just try again…And why don't you try…that spot over there, Doc…Threw an old tree trunk in there…makes another good hangout…for the bass…" With Clifford's guidance and some beginner's luck, I hooked a good-sized bass on my fourth or fifth cast, nearly lost it once when it jumped and nearly lost it again when it tail-walked across the pond, then finally brought it safely to shore. Clifford nodded approvingly and studied the bass closely, squinting through his reading glasses as I held it up by its lower lip. "You caught George," he said.

"You name your fish?" I asked.

"Sure do," Clifford replied. "They all look different, you know…See that notch right there…in the dorsal fin…and the way that black stripe on…the left side…takes a little turn there…there's only one like that in the pond…and that would be George." Clifford smiled at George fondly, and realizing that this gnarly old fish enjoyed the status of a pet or perhaps even an old family friend, I returned him to the pond gently, keeping a supportive hand under his belly until he recovered his breath (more quickly than Clifford, it seemed) and swam away with an unconcerned flick of his tail that might have been a casual goodbye wave.

We moved from the bass pond to the catfish pond as game time approached. Clifford tossed a handful of fish food pellets

into the pond, and a few dozen well-fed catfish instantly materialized at our feet. "Pick a nice fat one…for our dinner," huffed Clifford, who was clearly less attached to his catfish than he was to his bass. He baited a hook with a food pellet and handed me the rod; I dipped the pellet in front of a particularly large and unfortunate catfish, who about ten seconds later was flopping around on the weedy bank and in another fifteen minutes had been transformed into a steaming plateful of sweet and flaky deep-fried filets, served by Loretta along with hush puppies, biscuits, and greens just as Whitney Houston soared through the national anthem and the New York Giants kicked off to the Buffalo Bills.

The war, thankfully, ended almost as quickly as our brief Mississippi winter. Magnolia blossoms returned early that spring - and so did Larry, on a warm Thursday in March. Nan entered my office that afternoon with her usual cat-like stealth, but instead of slamming the next chart onto my desk, she waited until I looked up and then handed it to me with an uncharacteristic look of concern on her face. "Larry's back," she said. "And he doesn't look good."

It took me a moment to realize that the pile of baggy clothes on the examining table contained Larry's emaciated frame. He was lying on his right side, eyes closed as he concentrated on his labored breathing. Luanne looked up at me and shook her head.

"Hey Doc," Larry panted when I walked to the bedside and put a hand on his bony shoulder. "Sorry I deserted you." He took a few more breaths and then added, "Didn't find him. Don't care no more, neither."

"It's okay, Larry," I replied. "I'm just glad to see you."

That was the end of our conversation. Larry clearly had pneumonia, and I didn't want him to waste his breath talking. Luanne took him to the hospital while I called admitting orders to the medical floor.

"Lobar pneumonia," said Ruben Silva, one of our radiologists, later that afternoon as he pointed at a hazy area just to the right of Larry's cardiac silhouette. It occurred to me that I had only seen Ruben in the sickly blue and white fluorescent lighting of his cave-like film room; it would be startling to see him in living color. "Not great, but at least I don't think your guy has Pneumocystis."

Deb Harper, one of our soft-spoken young nurses, was hanging a bag of IV antibiotics when I entered Larry's room. Larry was still panting and barely looked wider than his oxygen tubing. I pulled Deb aside to make sure she understood the gravity of Larry's illness. "We'll all do our best for him," she reassured me in her soothing voice. "He's such a sweet boy. We'll treat him like he's one of our own."

Larry's first week in the hospital was a real struggle, but by the time I discharged him two weeks later, he had grown stronger and regained some of his lost weight, due in small part to his discovery of Ensure, which he drank by the case, and in larger part to the nurses, who true to Deb's promise had given Larry lots of tender loving care and even read books to him. His cough, though, was never to leave him.

When I saw Larry the following Thursday, he had managed to hang onto most of his regained weight, but his face had lost its last vestige of baby fat, as if the pneumonia had melted away whatever was left of his childhood. Always quiet, he now weighed his words even more carefully, and the hints of playful curiosity that I used to see in his eyes had given way to grave thoughtfulness. He reminded me of the pensive young John Coltrane as captured on the cover of his legendary "Blue Train" album. I avoided talking about basketball, mindful that Larry had disappeared to Memphis after my Bill Russell story, but he brought up the subject himself when I asked if he was feeling well enough to get some exercise. "I might try to shoot a few hoops," he said, "but I'd have to do it by myself now. My roundball buddies don't want to hang with me anymore because I have AIDS." He tossed out this remark very casually, but I noticed that it was the only moment during our visit that he avoided making eye contact with me.

Larry's wardrobe changed after his hospitalization; gone were the baggy sweatshirts and even his beloved Magic Johnson basketball shoes, replaced by button-down Oxford shirts and well-polished loafers. When I complimented Larry on his new look, he shrugged and said, "My old clothes were just getting too loose, so Luanne bought me some new stuff."

Larry's baggy jeans were gone, too, replaced by designer khakis, the latest trend in men's fashion. I tended to wear designer khakis myself, having found them to be very comfortable work clothes. "Nice pants, Doc," Larry would nod approvingly. "Dockers? That's what I'm wearing."

I would twist around, trying to see the logo above my right back pocket. "Nope," I might reply. "Nautica."

"Nice," Larry would say with another nod. "Gotta get me a pair."

Larry's Dockers and my Nauticas notwithstanding, the most fashionable people to set foot in the clinic were the pharmaceutical reps, who in addition to being sharp dressers were often as good-looking as movie stars. One of the reps who called most often, Dave Poirier, was also a neighbor from our apartment complex (and a Warren Beatty look-alike). After a while, Dave dropped his sales pitch and just stopped by to say hello and leave large numbers of drug samples, none of which ever went to waste. He dropped in one Thursday afternoon, just after Larry had left, and asked if we needed anything. I was a bit preoccupied, being concerned that Larry was starting to lose weight again, and talking mostly to myself muttered that I had an AIDS patient who could use some Ensure. "We don't make Ensure," Dave said, "but I know a place where I can get some. Let me see what I can do." True to his word, Dave showed up the next week with the trunk of his car stuffed to the weather stripping with cases of Ensure. I found out later that Dave had driven all the way to Louisiana to pick up the drinks, and when I started to thank him for going so far out of his way to help one of my patients, he held up his hand to stop me. "You and I might live in the same complex," he said, "but down here, we're all neighbors." Dave promised to make a monthly run to Louisiana on Larry's behalf, and he never let us down.

Just as our medicine closet overflowed with free drug samples, so did the New Orleans Saints mug on my desk overflow with free drug company pens. I noticed Mr. Leroy admiring my pen collection one day, he and his trusty push-broom standing in rare repose and his whistler resting in even rarer silence. "Pardon me, Doctor," Leroy apologized when I walked into the room. "I'll just get a move-on here."

"That's okay, Leroy," I reassured him. "Do you need a pen? Help yourself. I have more than I could ever use."

"Well, Doctor," Leroy said, "there is one that I wouldn't mind borrowing if you won't be needing it this weekend. I've been invited to preach on Sunday, you see, and I thought this one here would look right smart in my breast pocket."

I held up my Saints mug for Leroy, and with great care and ceremony he picked out a pen with the name of the latest anti-inflammatory drug emblazoned across its faux-marble casing. "That's a nice one," I said. "Keep it, please."

Leroy clipped the pen in his shirt pocket with an appreciative nod. "If you won't be missing it, then I thank you," he said. "I should be able to write a smart sermon, seeing as I'll be using a doctor's pen."

A tattered, leather-bound Bible, opened to a picture of David's battle with Goliath, sat on Larry's lap when I walked into the examining room one afternoon. "Are you on your way to church?" I asked. Larry, in addition to his now-customary button-down shirt and khakis, was also sporting a necktie, which along with his well-worn Bible gave him the look of an earnest young missionary.

"No," Larry replied. "I was just at a meeting with Pastor Eugene." I raised my eyebrows inquiringly, and he explained, "After church last week Pastor Eugene asked me to come see him. So I went today, and he told me that some of the folks are scared to have me around. He said if that made me uncomfortable maybe just the two of us could meet every week."

"That's terrible," I said. "Hey, if you want to go to church, you should go."

"Aw, it's all right, Doc," Larry mumbled. "Never been crazy about going to church anyway."

Leroy leaned thoughtfully on his push broom when I mentioned Larry's situation later that day. "That's not how I would minister if I had my own flock," he mused, "but I can't judge Pastor Eugene, not without walking in his shoes. Might be he's trying to protect Larry. There's a lot of folks out there that's scared of people with AIDS, you know, including some right fine Christians." Leroy thought for another moment before asking, "Would that be the young man who comes in Thursday afternoons? Well, I'll tell you what, Doc. Maybe next week the trash barrel in your examining room will need to be emptied on Thursday right after lunch. If that be okay with you, of course."

Leroy was tidying my office and whistling his little four bar melody when I stepped out of my examining room the following Thursday afternoon. He gave me a pleasant nod and rolled his trash barrel across the hallway. "Hello there, young fella," I heard him say, and then his voice faded to a more distant murmur. Fifteen minutes later, Nan stuck her head in my office door and whispered, "Did you put Mr. Leroy up to this?" When I confessed, she shook her head and sighed, "Don't you run far enough behind as it is?"

A few Thursdays later, I spotted an illustrated children's Bible peeking from Leroy's back pocket as he emptied my trash barrel. "I borrowed it from our Sunday School for Larry," Leroy explained, pulling the book from his pocket to show me its well-worn pages. "He doesn't read so well, you know." I suddenly recalled how the nurses at the hospital had read books to Larry and realized that he had been studying the picture of David and Goliath, rather than the text, the day I saw him looking at his Bible. "In the beginning..." I heard Leroy murmur across the hall.

We were by then into another sultry Mississippi summer, and I was so glad to get away on my first free summer weekend that I didn't even mind spending it in a New Orleans nursing home. The Air Force had arranged for Jane to do a rotation at the Ochsner Clinic, and the travel office booked her a hotel room near the Audubon Zoo. We loved the zoo and its surrounding area and thought the whole arrangement sounded lovely. Jane was despondent, though, when she called me on her first night in New Orleans; the "hotel", it turned out, was actually a nursing home. "Well, look on the bright side," I tried to console her. "We can make all the noise we want when I come to see you, and nobody will be able to hear us."

"That's not funny," she said.

I headed straight from my office to New Orleans on the following steamy Friday afternoon, grateful to be driving against the long lines of traffic headed for the beaches of Alabama and the Florida panhandle. The sky was a dusky, hazy purple by the time I walked into the lobby of the nursing home. It seemed an unlikely place to find Jane, but then I saw her weaving her way toward me through a maze of wheelchairs and their elderly occupants. "They really are hard of hearing," Jane observed in an unnecessary whisper as she led me back through the wheelchairs.

"Good thing," I whispered back.

Jane and I were newlyweds that summer, and during those long Friday afternoon drives I enjoyed lingering on the thought that I was going to New Orleans to see not my girlfriend but my wife. After I moved to Biloxi, Jane and I had on more than one occasion considered eloping to the Wedding Chapel, a miniature black raspberry-colored gingerbread house with a justice of the peace waving from the front porch, and then slipping next door to Hog Heaven, another neighborhood establishment which we had eyed many times but never quite dared enter, for a convenient and affordable post-wedding meal. When it was finally time to get married, though, the gravitational pull of a traditional wedding proved inescapable, and so it was that we found ourselves standing at the altar of a graceful New England church one crisp and perfect New England afternoon.

Jane's month at Ochsner passed quickly, and for the rest of the summer most of my Friday afternoons were spent not driving to New Orleans but attending clinic cookouts. "Let's go cool off," one of the secretaries would say at around three-ish, and we'd close the doors a little early and head to a nearby park. I never understood how abandoning our air-conditioned office for the blazing August sun and a flaming barbecue pit constituted "cooling off", but my co-workers always acted as if we were picnicking on a breezy Alpine ridge. I must have looked uncomfortably warm, though, because Sam would always find me a spot on the shade-speckled side of a scrubby little pine tree. "Come sit, Doc," he insisted, "it's at least five degrees cooler over here. And just bre-e-e-eathe…You can practically smell all the oxygen coming out of that tree, can't you?" I mimicked Sam's oxygen-inhaling demonstration as faithfully as I could and nodded my enthusiastic agreement, though all I could ever really smell was smoke, as Sam invariably positioned me just downwind from the barbecue pit.

Sam had always treated me with consideration and respect but did so even more now that I was the clinic's medical director. It had been a season of change. Barbara Morgan had been the first to leave. She always wanted to care for those who needed her most, and as I settled into the job and the plight of our patients became less desperate, Barbara decided to focus solely on her prison work. I missed hearing Barbara's high heels on the linoleum floor, not because I longed for the extra work that often trailed her oncoming footsteps but because I had come to value and respect her unstoppable determination.

Clay Cooper was no longer with us, either, though it took a while to realize that he was gone for good. His behavior had been erratic ever since the morning his medical assistant Lucia shouted, "It be someone from Oklahoma on the phone, Dr. Cooper!" Clay ran down the hall yelling, "I'm not here!" and then locked himself in his office.

"He says he not be here," Lucia informed the caller. The calls continued for the next few weeks, as did the increasingly familiar sound of Clay's frantic footsteps and the thunderous slamming of his office door. The last time I saw Clay was during one of our occasional brown bag lunches together; eyes red-rimmed and puffy with sleeplessness, he went on a bitter, Dr. Pepper-fueled rant about blood-sucking divorce lawyers, left-wing conspiracies, and his somewhat vague hatred of Texans. Then one day he didn't come to work; the day stretched to a week, two weeks, and then a month, at which point we finally accepted that we no longer had a pediatrician.

It was Lamar Blackwell's departure, though, that propelled me into the medical director's position. I was never quite sure why Lamar left, but he seemed more pressured than ever in his final few months. Lamar hoarded more and more charts, until the nurses and secretaries would send stacks of notes and lab reports crashing to the floor every time they tried to maneuver through his dimly lit office. The stacks eventually grew so high that we couldn't see Lamar when he sat at his desk, and conversing with him had become rather like calling to someone trapped at the bottom of a deep, dark well. Then one day Lamar drove away, taking with him a trunk full of charts, and we never saw him again (though to Sam's everlasting astonishment the charts did reappear months later, left in neat stacks on the floor of the medical records room by some mysterious middle of the night visitor).

The president of the board of trustees showed up in my office not long afterward. "The clinic needs a new medical director," she said.

"I noticed," I replied.

"You're the only doctor here now," she pointed out.

"I noticed that, too," I said.

"How are you at administrative work?"

"Terrible."

"How are you at running meetings?"

"Even worse."

"Congratulations," she said, rising to shake my hand. "The job's yours."

I dragged my feet about organizing our first meeting, but running it turned out to be much easier than I anticipated. Lamar had not convened us for many months, and people started to air out nearly a year's worth of grievances as soon as we sat down. I tried several times to interject my carefully prepared opening remarks into the growing commotion, but doing so was like trying to wade into a raging river after a torrential rainstorm. Fortunately, I had with unintentional brilliance scheduled the meeting during one of our pot-luck lunch Fridays, for the shouting ended as abruptly as it had begun, everyone having settled their differences and run to the lunchroom once they realized that the hour to savor Miss Sandy's flaky biscuits and Miss Melanie's sweet gravy had nearly expired. Sam gave me a thumbs-up and mumbled, "Great job, Doc!" through a mouthful of jambalaya, even though I hadn't uttered a single word the entire time.

The sizzling summer of departures cooled off into a refreshing autumn, but that, too, proved to be a season of change. Nan moved down the hall to pediatrics, though she assured me that I was not the reason she was leaving. "It's because of that poster," she explained. "You know, the one with the dog in the bathtub? They don't need those posters in pediatrics, if you know what I mean." She left me with one of her trademark flurries of ambiguous gestures, shrugging her shoulders, wrinkling her nose, shaking her head, and saying "Mm hmm" all at the same time. I thought it would be fun for a change to see Nan pounce in her feline fashion on another doctor, but when I heard that our new pediatrician had been coaxed out of a long retirement I began to fear that the sound of chart meeting desk would be followed by the sound of senior citizen meeting floor. I needn't have worried, though; Harriet Turner was too locked into her own tranquil rhythms, and perhaps too hard of hearing, to be the least bit troubled by Nan's cat-and-mouse antics. Harriet embodied the folksiness to which I felt Clay had always aspired but never quite achieved. A child with a fever was "burning like a barn afire", and an adolescent going through a growth spurt was "stretching for the sky like a Kansas cornstalk." Even a simple "How are you, Dr. Turner?" was met with a firmly declared "Fitter than a row of bass fiddles!" I eventually deciphered most of Harriet's seemingly endless supply of aphorisms but remained forever baffled by her ability to move so slowly yet still see so many patients. The economy of her movements reminded me of those Saturday afternoon horror films in which the monster lumbering with unbent knees through the forest still catches the beautiful and extremely fit young damsel who has been fleeing from him like a cheetah.

My new medical assistant, Claire, moved just as quietly as Nan, but she did so with delicacy rather than stealth, and the charts started to appear on rather than explode onto my desk. While I was already familiar with Claire's quietly thoughtful ways from her days as Barbara Morgan's medical assistant - she often stopped by after one of Barbara's tornado-like trips through my office to help me sort through the rubble - I hadn't anticipated the small ways in which she would bring more order to my day.

For instance, I had many times gone through the futile exercise of asking Sam to bring all of my lab reports at the same time, only to have him shuffle into my office, stray reports in his hands and expressions of chagrin on his lips, more often than ever. Claire, understanding better than I did that Sam would never manage to change his ways, quietly started to intercept Sam's frequent missives, and one afternoon I found two neat stacks on my desk; one consisted of normal lab results, and the other consisted of abnormal results, each of the latter clipped to the appropriate patient chart. When I thanked Claire, she responded by apologizing for not also pulling the charts that went along with the normal results. I told her that wasn't a problem and thanked her again. Even so, the next day she started pulling those charts, too, and kept them handy on her desk, just in case I needed them.

Claire liked cozy spaces and at lunchtime would curl up in her desk chair and read thrillers, many of them of the medical variety. She sometimes sought my opinion of the implausible plot lines, asking, for instance, if it were really possible that a corrupt hospital executive would conspire with an even more corrupt cardiothoracic surgeon to transplant hearts in secret from kidnapped homeless people into wealthy but weak-hearted hospital patrons. I read a couple of Claire's medical thrillers, at her urging, and felt a bit inadequate for bearing so little resemblance to the dashing Dr. Watson-James Bond superhero hybrids who populated that genre. "I don't think I could hot-wire a helicopter and fly it through surface-to-air missile fire with one hand while concocting a vaccine for a deadly African virus with the other," I confessed to Claire one day as I handed back her latest best-seller.

"Oh, I'm sure you could if you had to," she replied sweetly.

In spite of her quieter manners, Claire did have at least two things in common with Barbara Morgan: they were both single moms, having rid themselves of alcoholic husbands, and they were both tougher than they looked. Claire's ex-husband, who she described as "a good man inside a no-good drunk's body", came to bother her and their young daughter, Holly, in a drunken state one time too many, and Claire chased him off for good with a shotgun. "Don't worry, it warn't loaded," she reassured me when I expressed my aversion to firearms. "Too bad I didn't find that out, though, until he was high-tailing it down the driveway and I tried to shoot a round over his head. Dang!"

"Claire," I made her promise, "if you ever get mad at me, we'll just talk, right?"

Claire also proved to be an astute clinician and on at least one occasion handed me the right diagnosis before I even had a chance to meet the patient. "Jethro Paul has sleep apnea," she declared one morning as she placed another chart on my desk.

"Why do you say that?" I asked.

"Because he keeps falling asleep while I'm talking to him," Claire answered. "Patty Paul insists that her husband has caught sleeping sickness from a tse-tse fly, but I had an uncle who used to do what Jethro's doing, and he was diagnosed with sleep apnea. I'd never heard of sleep apnea, but I'm sure you know all about it, don't you?"

"Of course I do," I replied with feigned confidence. I stood by the examining room door pretending to study Jethro Paul's chart, but in truth I was wracking my brains to recall even the most elementary clinical features of sleep apnea. Sleep medicine was a relatively new field at the time, and while I had learned about sleep apnea as a resident, I had never actually encountered it in a patient and was frankly a bit skeptical that a sleeping person would cease to breathe for long stretches of the night. Sleep apnea patients snore, I remembered; heavy soft palates, thick-set necks, and daytime sleepiness gradually emerged into recollection, too. Nothing else would come to mind, so I knocked on the door and entered the room. As I did so Jethro Paul's head snapped up, a movement so abrupt and violent that it almost launched him over the back of his chair and shook his eyes into a furious fit of blinking. Jethro's temporary disorientation offered me a moment of observation. He was built like a garden gnome; his thick, sloping neck, sensed as much as seen behind his bushy black beard, merged without any angles into his barrel-shaped torso, which in turn tapered into short and very thick arms and legs. "Caught me napping," Jethro drawled with a sleepy grin. "But that's why I'm here, Doc. My wife Patty swears I've been bitten by a tse-tse fly."

"Do you snore?" I asked.

Jethro shrugged. "Patty says I do a bit, but I don't believe her."

"Why not?" I asked, but Jethro didn't answer. He was asleep again.

Claire knocked on the door to inform me that Patty Paul wanted to join us. "Does Jethro snore?" I asked after she had smacked her husband on the side of his head to wake him up.

"Does he snore?" Patty exclaimed. "He makes the walls shake! And if it's not Jethro shaking the house, then it's our son Jacob."

"Do they ever stop breathing?" I asked.

Patty stared at me, eyes wide with amazement. "Now how on earth did you ever know that?" she replied.

Patty told me that Jacob was napping in the waiting room, and I asked Claire to retrieve him. I had suspected that Jacob would resemble Jethro but wasn't prepared to see such an exact gnome-like replica, albeit on a smaller scale and minus the bushy black beard. Father and son sat side by side and conversed with me in tag-team fashion, one of them answering my questions while the other slept, then flip-flopping their roles seamlessly. "Have you ever in your life seen anything like it?" Patty asked with an exasperated shake of her head.

A quick examination of Jethro and Jacob revealed the likely cause of their sleep apnea; their soft palates were so heavy and their tonsils so large that breathing for them must have been like sucking air through a straw. They might benefit from surgery, eventually, but in the meantime I got Seymour Baker, a neurologist who was trying to establish a sleep lab at the hospital, to loan the Pauls some used breathing machines in exchange for their agreement to test some of his new equipment. The machines were remarkably effective; Jethro turned out to be very pleasant company, now that he could stay awake long enough for a real conversation, and Jacob, in the words of Harriet Turner, could suddenly "run about like a chicken after a handful of feed".

Larry and Claire quickly became very close. Larry, who had always been intimidated by Nan, felt very comfortable with Claire, and Claire adopted Larry as her younger brother. It was no surprise, then, that Larry came immediately to Claire's mind when Sam, who always passed along news from the records room radio like a town crier, popped his head in the door to tell us that Magic Johnson had been diagnosed with HIV. "He's going to be crushed," Claire sighed, knowing that she didn't have to specify to whom she was referring.

I thought Larry might bring up Magic Johnson's situation when he came to see me on Thursday afternoon, but he just sat impassively until I asked him if he had been upset by the news. Larry stared at the floor for a while, then looked up and said, "I always wanted to be just like Magic, but Magic turned out to be just like me."

I hadn't expected Larry to say something so bitter, but when I looked at him closely, searching for the hardened edge that might have accompanied his words, I saw that he was still the same old Larry, earnest and somber, and I realized that he had spoken of his bond with Magic with neither bitterness nor irony but with quiet pride. The taste of bitterness was left instead for me as I wondered how life could be so cruel as to toss this undemanding young man such a meager scrap of comfort. And even this cold scrap came with a cruel twist, for while Magic was proclaiming that he would lead the world's fight against HIV and that he him-self would beat the disease, Larry was slowly but surely succumb-ing to this same virus, his T cell count drifting ever downward and the weight continuing to melt from his emaciated frame, no matter how many cans of Ensure he drank every day.

Larry had been my first AIDS patient, but by this time he had plenty of company. We didn't have an infectious disease specialist at the hospital, and almost all of the HIV patients in the county ended up with either Fred Stevenson, one of our hematologists, or myself. Fred and I used to confer once in a while during morning rounds to catch up on the latest treatment strategies. HIV researchers were on the cusp of developing new anti-retroviral drugs, delivered in complex regimens that would come to be known as "drug cocktails", which when combined with diligence and a dash of good luck held the promise of turning HIV into a chronic rather than a fatal disease - a remarkable and a remarkably swift accomplishment, given that HIV had been discovered just ten years earlier. As the new drugs were still in clinical trials, though, a minute or two was enough for Fred and me to reassure each other that the regimens we were using were still up to the standard of care.

It was difficult to explain to patients like Larry that Magic's bold predictions of a brighter future didn't apply to them, that the virus already had too much of a stranglehold on their immune systems, not to mention their brains and livers and hearts, for the new drugs coming out of the research pipeline to be of much use to them. It was difficult for me, that is; Larry and most of my other AIDS patients seemed to understand instinctively that the vitality seeping out of their bodies would not be regained.

Larry had to be hospitalized for pneumonia twice that winter and then again in the spring. I made sure that he got admitted to the same floor every time so he could see some familiar faces. Larry became particularly attached to soft-spoken Deb Harper, who fussed over Larry less than the other nurses but spent a lot of time quietly sitting beside his bed and occasionally reading books to him. Larry became well-known by some of my fellow doctors, too; Fred Stevenson, with whom I discussed Larry's case to get advice on antibiotic coverage, often stopped by his room to see how he was doing, and Barry Smith, the family practitioner who had shared call with me for the last year and a half, got to know Larry from weekend rounds. Interest in Larry's dramatic chest x-rays even prompted Ruben Silva to make a rare visit to the medical floor, where I finally got a glimpse of Ruben outside the fluorescent blue and white glow of his reading room, only to find that he was wearing a blue and white striped shirt and blue pants.

The colleague who got to know Larry best, though, was Travis Dupree, a solo practitioner who had just gotten his hospital privileges reinstated after maintaining sobriety for two years. Barry and I quickly became friendly with Travis when he started doing morning rounds, and we invited him to join our coverage rotation, which afforded us the luxury of being on call every third weekend. My first impression of Travis was that he came from a different century; with his long legs and lanky, Lincoln-esque frame, rugged loose-fitting work clothes, neat brown pony tail, quiet smile, and strong handshake, Travis had the air of a self-reliant pioneer, and his thirst for whiskey, along with the hand-rolled cigarettes which left him completing every other sentence with a light cough, made him seem even more like a figure from the old frontier. Travis had a way of putting people at ease, probably because he seemed so at ease with himself. He was candid and self-effacing about his drinking problem and once told Barry and me that his struggles with alcohol had in many ways been illuminating. His one great regret was that his drinking had caused so much hardship for his wife, Meredith, who I met once when I stopped by Travis's office. It was a tidy little space, and very quiet; Travis, having just recently reopened his practice, had few patients, and Meredith was for now helping him run the office. Meredith was a lovely, soft-spoken Southern belle whose worry lines made her seem delicate and vulnerable, especially when standing next to her rugged husband. It was touching to see the quietly considerate way Travis and Meredith treated each other; they were clearly a couple that had gone through some tough times but had gone through them together.

Morning rounds remained a hectic exercise of running from patient to patient, charting notes and orders, and escaping to the office, but it was a real pleasure once in a while to run into Barry and Travis on the floor and talk shop. Barry was a rock solid person and clinician, a methodical and logical thinker whose judgment I valued greatly. Travis, on the other hand, tended to connect his dots in a haphazard but sometimes brilliant fashion, peppering his commentary with an occasional reference to subjects I had never quite grasped. "You've got to be careful dosing that drug because it can cause type 2 renal tubular acidosis," he might say, before adding with a modest cough, "though I've pretty much forgotten all that stuff."

Because Travis's practice was still quite slow, he took his time on rounds and often spent most of his day at the hospital. The HIV epidemic had exploded during Travis's enforced leave of absence, and he spent hours in the hospital's small library catching up on the HIV literature. Travis offered to keep an eye on Larry whenever he was hospitalized, and I appreciated any help I could get from such a keen-eyed clinician. I think that Travis was, at first, most interested in Larry from an academic viewpoint. He soon became genuinely fond of Larry, though, and Larry in turn became very comfortable with Travis's friendly but laid-back manner.

Larry barely made it out of the hospital after his third bout of pneumonia. He sat in my office the following Thursday afternoon, looking tired and defeated. Larry no longer chugged Ensure, partly because he had lost faith in the power of extra nutrition and partly because of the thick layers of thrush which coated his throat but mostly because he had simply lost all interest in food. His formerly crisp Oxford shirts, now tattered and stained, hung loosely from his increasingly skeletal frame, and his frayed designer khakis were bunched at the waist, his well-polished brown leather belt having been replaced by a much shorter one made of shiny black vinyl. "Look at me, Doc," Larry said in a low, mournful tone, "having to wear a little boy's belt now."

I patted Larry on his bony shoulder, listened to his painfully weak and wheezy lungs, and then after taking a deep breath of my own broke the news that I would be leaving the clinic in another month and a half. Jane and I had throughout the short Gulf Coast winter unfurled on our dining room table a map of the world, its unruly ends pinned down by heavy medical textbooks, our eyes drawn with involuntary frequency to far-flung points of latitude and longitude - Ankara, Minot, Wiesbaden, Honolulu, Seoul, San Antonio - as she and her fellow senior residents awaited the assignment of their next tours of duty. The Air Force had nothing so exotic in mind for us, though; Jane informed me when she came home one March evening that she had been assigned to Walson Air Force Base in New Jersey as the new chief of pediatrics. I told her how impressed I was by her grand-sounding promotion. "Don't be," she replied in her typically modest way. "I'm going to be a department of one."

I had informed the clinic of my departure date right away and started sharing the news with my patients as they came in for their office visits. It felt strange to tell them to return in three months when as of yet no one had been found to take my place; while some worried about the uncertainty, most seemed to regard not having a doctor as a return to their natural state of affairs, with my presence in their lives over the last two years having been an unexpected though not unwelcome interlude.

I had, however, passed up many opportunities to tell Larry that I was leaving. I told Claire that I was just waiting for Larry to recover from his latest bout of pneumonia before giving him the news. The grimmer truth, though, was that it didn't look like Larry would outlast my remaining time in Mississippi, and I thought our reticence might spare him from a feeling of abandonment. Claire also had news from which she had been shielding Larry. She and I never spoke of it openly, but we both knew that Larry, who had looked up to Claire like a big sister when they first met, had since then formed a much deeper attachment to her. Larry used to chat with Claire in what was for him a talkative manner; over the next few months he became much quieter in Claire's presence, looking at her with grave sweetness and inquiring about her well-being with gentlemanly formality, and when he was in the hospital our daily visit was never finished until he asked, "Hey Doc, how Claire be doing?" Claire knew that Larry would be crushed to learn that she and her boyfriend, Pete, a mechanic at one of the local car dealerships, were getting married, and so she, too, had remained silent about her plans until this warm Thursday afternoon in May, when through some unspoken synchrony of thought Claire and I both came to the reluctant conclusion that it was unfair not to let Larry know about the changes coming into our lives and therefore into his life as well.

"So Claire be getting married," Larry said, as if he hadn't even heard me say that I was moving to New Jersey.

"Yes," I replied, adding with good intentions but perhaps with cruel effect, "Pete's a good man."

"I'm glad," Larry said in a low voice. "Claire deserves a good man."

"You're a good man, too, as good as any," I declared. "But things don't always work out the way we wish, even for the best of us."

"You know what, Doc, nothing in my whole life has ever worked out the way I wished," Larry sighed. "I've given up on wishes. I've just plain given up."

"Don't give up, Larry," I said. "There's always hope."

"Hope for what?" asked Larry. "Magic promised he was going to find me a cure, but he was wrong. I'm going to die soon, I can just feel it creeping up on me."

Larry's question was one I always dreaded; what was there to hope for, indeed, when a slowly dying patient's long retreat had finally reached its bitter end and all was clearly lost? I started to recite my standard speech about hope, but as I gazed upon this wasted and heartbroken young man those well-practiced lines suddenly seemed like such hollow psychobabble that they stuck in my throat. In the long ensuing silence, one that was broken only by the rhythmic ticking of my watch and the less rhythmic wheezing of Larry's lungs, I held out my own hope to the wind – hope that other words, more helpful than those I had been about to say, would find their way to me.

"You're right, Larry, there's not a miracle cure on the way," I finally conceded. "But we can still hope that tomorrow will bring something good, maybe some small thing that we weren't expecting. And when we finally run out of tomorrows we can still hope for good things for the people we've left behind."

Larry nodded thoughtfully at the floor. An almost-smile that seemed to say Nice try Doc flickered across his somber features, and when he looked up his moment of self-pity, the last one - indeed, the only one - I would ever witness, had passed. "Okay," Larry said, "I'll tell you what. I'll make one last wish - that my dad's been a good man all these years, so maybe I'll get to meet him someday."

"Then I'll wish for that, too," I said.

"And Doc," Larry added, "I'm going to miss you when you go to New Jersey. You been good to me, and I been glad for that, 'cause you know what, there ain't enough kindness in the world."

Larry passed away two weeks later. I was away at the time, much to my regret, having gone with Jane to New Jersey to visit Walson Air Force Base and find both a new apartment and, for me, a new job. Travis Dupree called me shortly after we returned on Sunday night to give me the news. Luanne had brought Larry to the clinic on Friday afternoon, and Claire, recognizing that Larry was gravely ill, had called to see if Travis would admit him. Leroy helped transport Larry to the hospital, where Travis with a single glance saw that Larry was about to die and simply put him on fluids, oxygen, and morphine. Luanne, he said, never left Larry's side, and Deb Harper was there to take care of him, too, until he passed away quietly on Saturday afternoon. "It was my pleasure," Travis said when I thanked him for taking care of Larry at the end. "He sure was a nice young fellow." The line went silent for a moment, and then Travis added, after starting with one of his trademark coughs, "There was just something about Larry that made you feel a little better about yourself." There was more silence and then another cough. "You know, Meredith forgave me a long time ago for my drinking. Maybe I'll work on forgiving myself one of these days, too."

Larry's funeral was, fittingly, on Thursday afternoon at one. Reverend Eugene's church was just a few blocks from the clinic, but I was still one of the last to arrive, having in my usual fashion run behind schedule all morning. Sounds of weeping, wailing, and moaning met my ears when I got out of my car and grew louder as I crossed the parking lot toward the flat-roofed one-story meeting hall. When I entered the cool, dim sanctuary I realized

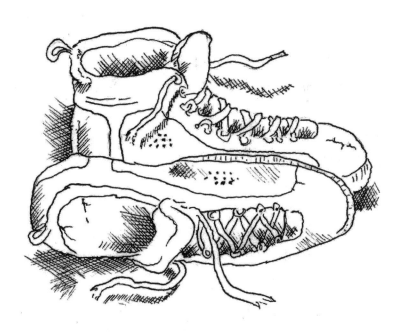

that while some of the wails and moans were wordless, most were repetitive utterances of "Brother Larry".

Reverend Eugene offered Larry a stirring eulogy and reassured us that he had gone to a better rest with the Lord, a reassurance that was met with many amens, hallelujahs, and Brother Larrys. As the call and response between Reverend Eugene and his congregation reached its climax, so too did my slowly growing anger as I questioned where all of these people had been when the hollow-cheeked young man lying before us in his shiny new black suit had needed them most. I wasn't alone in my anger; at one point Luanne glanced back from her seat in the front pew and caught my eye with a bitter smile and a quick, disbelieving shake of her head. My feelings must have been apparent, too, for as I paid my respects to Reverend Eugene after the service he said, "We didn't really desert Brother Larry, you know. There were just a few brothers and sisters who felt uncomfortable around him, but he was a proud young man, and that was enough to make him pull away from us. It will be to our everlasting shame, Doctor, that we left Brother Larry feeling so alone. Others in the community have AIDS now, and many more will follow, I'm afraid. We will do better."

I told Claire about Larry's funeral but otherwise didn't see much of her for the next week as she prepared for her wedding. Claire asked me to provide the music for her processional, so on the following extremely warm Saturday afternoon I dusted off my saxophone and stood in the shade of a Spanish moss-laden oak tree on her mother's front lawn and played Kurt Weill's "Lost in the Stars" as Claire walked through the gathering of guests and took Pete's hand. Afterward, as we drank punch on the shady front porch and watched Claire and Pete open their wedding presents, one of Pete's fellow mechanics came up to Jane and me and said in the slowest Southern drawl that I had yet heard in my two years in Mississippi, every syllable drawn out to the length of a New York paragraph, "A saxophone playing doctor. My, my, my, now I have seen everything there is to see!"

The late afternoon sun filtered softly through the old oak tree's verdant canopy as Jane and I offered our congratulations to Claire and Pete. "Larry would have been happy for you," I said, "in spite of it all."

"Yes," Claire agreed. "Yes, he sure would."

We passed a Sonic Burger drive-in on the way home, and Jane, whose tastes didn't usually run toward greasy hamburgers, surprised me by insisting that we stop there for dinner. The punch at Claire's wedding, I figured, must have given her an appetite for something different. About halfway through our dripping half-pound cheeseburgers, though, Jane suddenly looked ill; she groaned and slumped over, and I was alarmed both by her sudden pallor and by the possibility that she was about to

ruin my Mustang's upholstery. "We shouldn't have eaten here," I complained.

Jane lifted her head weakly. "It's not the food," she said, and in the pause which followed I suddenly understood how much our lives were about to change. "I'm pregnant."

Mississippi didn't let go of us easily. There were farewell lunches and dinners in those final two weeks (a struggle for Jane because of her relentless morning sickness) with people whose friendship had come to mean more to us than we had realized, and with a surprising sense of urgency we visited some of our favorite local spots for the last time - from the pizza buffet, where Jane and I had puzzled over the sugar-dusted dessert pizzas while the waitresses puzzled over our puzzlement, to the unguarded and modestly mourned Tomb of the Unknown Confederate Soldier in the shady yard behind Jefferson Davis's house - spots that we didn't even know had become favorites until it was time to leave them behind. Claire came back from her honeymoon on my last day at the office, and we spent the afternoon organizing charts for my replacement, a doctor who was just finishing her family practice internship somewhere in the Caribbean. Claire and I finally had everything wrapped up and were struggling to find the right words of appreciation for each other when Sam came shuffling in with one last lab report. "Sorry, Doc," he said, "found another one!"

"Too late!" we both laughed, and Sam's shuffling footsteps and good-humored protests were the last sounds I heard as I slipped out the back door of the clinic.

The day of our departure was hot, even by Mississippi standards. I packed the car, trying to keep Jane in our air-conditioned apartment as long as possible; then we bade farewell to our first home and turned in our keys. We made a quick stop at the grocery store to buy some provisions for the trip, only to find that my Mustang, the trusty steed which had borne me safely from Boston to Mississippi and through a thousand triangular journeys from home to hospital to clinic and then home again, had died in the parking lot, worn out at last by the Southern heat. Our unfailingly cheerful grocery store manager invited Jane to rest in his air-conditioned office while I got the car towed to the garage.

"Car's a bit tired," said the mechanic three hours later. "I've fixed her up enough to get you where you're going, but she'll need big repairs when you get there. Just remember that if you step on the brake too hard the engine's going to stall. So my advice is to keep your foot on the gas pedal and don't look back."

And that's exactly what I did, at least until we drove eastward over the Pascagoula River and approached the Alabama border. I stole a quick glance at Jane just as her long brown eyelashes were fluttering into well-earned and much-needed sleep, her duty as a doctor and an officer done and done well and her life as a mother just beginning. Then I took a glance in the rear-view mirror for one last look at Mississippi. The sun was low in the summer sky, and across the heavy reddish haze on the western horizon drifted many shadows, shadows of Howard Thurmond and Bob Harmon sitting with me all night at Earl Crosby's bedside, of Rosie Jordan's crinkly-eyed smile as she handed me another one of her little treasures, of Mr. Leroy pushing his broom with a smile on his face and a child's Bible in his back pocket, of Dave Poirier staggering into our clinic with crates of Ensure stacked high in his arms, of Sam trying to find me a shady spot with plenty of oxygen, of Deb Harper holding Larry's hand as she read him a book, of the pride on Travis Dupree's face when he looked at Meredith…Echoes I heard, too, drifting toward me across the limpid steel-blue waters of the Gulf, echoes of nurses chiding Diane Johnson ever so gently for her wayward wanderings, of Claire in her sweet unassuming voice reassuring Larry that he would always be her little brother, of Barbara Morgan's high heels clicking with untamable optimism toward another lost soul, of the clinic staff praising Miss Sandy's flaky biscuits as if they were tasting them for the first time…and then came the last echo of all, a whisper faint but indelible, the echo of Larry's final words to me.

There ain't enough kindness in the world, Larry had said.

But maybe there is, I wanted to tell him. Maybe there is.

ABOUT THE AUTHOR

Jeff Wu is an internist in Boston, Massachusetts and lives in the Boston area with his wife and their two sons. *A Last Wish for Larry* is his first published work of fiction.

Made in the USA
Middletown, DE
15 July 2015